Penny Dreadful
and the School Inspector

Penny Dreadful's
Top 5 Tips for Survival

Meet Penny Dreadful and her Resigned Relations

Penny
(It's never really her fault…)

Georgia May Morton-Jones
(Penny's clever cousin)

Cosmo
(Penny's now-very-bald best friend)

Daisy
(Penny's annoying sister)

Penny's longsuffering mum and dad

Very prim-and-proper Aunt Deedee

Barry
(Miaow, I'm Gran's cat)

Gran
(Normally found fast asleep somewhere)

Penny Dreadful

Dreadful

Becomes a
Hairdresser

My name is not actually Penny Dreadful.

It is Penelope Jones. The "Dreadful" bit is my dad's **JOKE**. I know it is a joke because every time he says it he laughs like a honking goose. But I do not see the funny side. Plus it is not even true that I am dreadful. It is like Gran says, i.e. that I am a **MAGNET FOR DISASTER**. Mum says if Gran kept a better eye on me in the first place instead of on *Cheese and Biscuits* in the two o'clock at Newmarket then I might not be quite so magnetic. But Gran says if Mum wasn't so busy answering phones for Dr. Cement, who is her boss and who has bulgy eyes like hard-boiled eggs (which is why everyone calls him Dr. Bugeye), and Dad wasn't so busy solving crises at the council, then they would be able to solve some crises at 73 Rollins Road, i.e. our house. So you see it is completely not my fault.

⭐ ☆ ✦ ✯

Anyway when I get up this morning I am full of gloom even though it is the holidays because of several things, i.e.:

1. My sister Daisy, who is eleven, and very irritating, is doubly irritating because she is going to Monkey Madness tomorrow and is pleased as punch.

b. I am not allowed to go to Monkey Madness because Mum says there is too much **POTENTIAL FOR CATASTROPHE**, plus it costs £8.75 and I still owe her £7.50 for the time I accidentally phoned India.

3. There are no Sugar Pops left for breakfast because Gran's cat Barry has eaten the last bowlful, even though Mum has told Gran that Barry is supposed to eat **CAT BISCUITS AND CAT BISCUITS ONLY**.

But then it gets completely worse because the door goes and it is Aunt Deedee who is dropping off Georgia May Morton-Jones, i.e. my cousin, because she has a **CRUCIAL MEETING WITH THE NEW YORK BOYS** and has sacked Katya Romanov (who is the au pair) for **NOT MEASURING UP**. Aunt Deedee is Dad's sister, although Gran says sometimes she thinks she brought the wrong baby back from the hospital because she is not at all like Dad, i.e. she does not ever wear creased trousers or drink orange juice from the carton (which Mum says is unhygienic but everyone does it, even Daisy). Plus Aunt Deedee is always sacking au pairs for **NOT MEASURING UP**. Although Gran says not even the Queen of Sheba would **MEASURE UP** in Aunt Deedee's eyes.

Anyway Mum says she is working all day because Dr. Cement has a verruca clinic and Dad is at the council solving a crisis to do with some bollards so Gran is in charge. Then Aunt Deedee's eyes go a bit thin and squinty because she is not keen on Gran being in charge ever since the time she let Georgia May Morton-Jones eat mud because she said it would give her the **CONSTITUTION OF AN OX**, but as Gran says **BEGGARS CAN'T BE CHOOSERS** so Aunt Deedee says,

Fine, but there is to be absolutely no messy play, no eating dirt and, Penelope Jones, if you even think of persuading Georgia May Morton-Jones to run away to the North Pole again I will quite possibly spontaneously combust.

I say I am too gloomy to run away, even
though seeing Aunt Deedee spontaneously
combust would be quite interesting. Aunt Deedee
says "Good" and then goes back to shouting in
her phone at someone called Henrietta.

But now I am even more gloomy because
Georgia May Morton-Jones is here all day
and she is only four and a bit and not usually
interested in any of my **BRILLIANT IDEAS**™
in case she ruins her clothes or her fingers, which
are very important because Mr. Nakamura says
she shows potential on the violin. I do not show
potential on the violin, although I did do
"Twinkle Twinkle Little Star" on the recorder at
the Festive Jamboree last year and I only got
five notes wrong.

13

So what happens is we have to play snap all morning until Gran makes us corned beef sandwiches for lunch, only Georgia May has cheese because she says the corned beef looks like cat food and she is not allowed cat food after last time. And I am just thinking that I might die of boredom when the door goes again. Gran says "It is like Piccadilly Circus round here", which Daisy says is not actually a circus with lions and trapeze at all, it is just a road with a lot of cars so Gran is wrong on all counts. But this time it is Cosmo

Webster, i.e. my best friend (even though he is a boy and exactly a week older, because neither of those things are his fault), and amazingly he has **NO HAIR**. Gran says,

Lawks a mussy, Cosmo, what happened to you?

Because normally Cosmo has hair that is even longer than mine.

Cosmo says, "It is because of the nits."

What has happened is that Cosmo's mum, who is called Sunflower even though her real name is Barbara, does not believe in chemicals or killing innocent insects, so she has tried to persuade the nits to leave by using a special chant. But the nits have not been listening and instead they multiplied like **MAD** and Cosmo's head was very itchy, so Sunflower said he had to get it cut, but she could not do it because **a)** her scissors are lost from when we used them as divining rods to find water under the roundabout, and **2.** hair is a sign of strength and she cannot be the one to **SAP HIS POWERS**.

So he has been to
Hair Today and
Shaniqua Reynolds
has cut it all off for £5.

   And that is when
I have the first

BRILLIANT IDEA™,

which is **TO BECOME A HAIRDRESSER,**
because I have worked out I only need to do
one and a bit haircuts to pay Mum back for
phoning India and then I will be able to
go to Monkey Madness with Daisy.
And Aunt Deedee did not say

NO HAIRDRESSING so it is fine.

17

So then me and Cosmo go into my office, i.e. my bedroom, and write a list of all the people we can give haircuts to and Georgia May comes too because Gran wants to watch *Animal SOS*, which is a TV series where animals are always nearly dying but then they don't and it is **MIRACULOUS**, and Georgia May is not allowed to watch TV unless it is the Maths Channel. By the time we have finished we have five people on our list, i.e.:

1. Gran

b. Barry. Even though he is a cat we will still charge £5 because he is very hairy and the bit on his bottom is tangled from when he sat on a piece of Cosmo's bubblegum.

3. Daisy

4. Bridget Grimes who is in our class and has very long hair that actually reaches her waist and she is always swishing it and saying "My hair actually reaches my waist, Penelope Jones", but Mum says it needs a jolly good cut.

e. Brady O'Grady who is also in our class but he has his head shaved every week, sometimes with patterns in it, so it will be an easy job.

And Cosmo has made a
notice out of the back of my
Dogs of the World poster
and a glitter pen and it
says **GET YOUR HARE
CUT HERE**, which looks
really **EYE-CATCHING**
even though Georgia
May points out it is
the wrong sort of
hare, but I say the
first rule of business is
being **EYE-CATCHING**
not spelling properly,
so we put the poster up
on my door and wait.

And then what happens
is that Daisy comes out
of her bedroom with
Lucy B. Finnegan
(who once got
her finger
stuck in the
plughole in our
bathroom) to see what
all the **FUSS** is about, and Daisy says,
"Penelope Jones, you are a **MORON** if you
think anyone will let you cut their hair."
And Lucy B. Finnegan says, "You've spelled
'hair' wrong, too." And then they are
killing themselves laughing, so we decide to go
to the shops to do our haircuts because it is too

distracting with all the
noise at home.
But when we
get to the shops
I realize I have
totally not got
any scissors because
they are in the
kitchen in the **OUT
OF BOUNDS** drawer after I used them to cut
up an old curtain for an emergency rope ladder
(only it wasn't an *old* curtain at all), and so
I am like a wizard without a wand. Cosmo says
we need to borrow some off somebody and I say
maybe we can ask Mrs. Butterworth at the post
office because even though she is always saying

ve got my beady eye on you"

a moustache, so I think we can offer

exchange for the scissors and our

collateral, which means our money, which is

23p that Cosmo found in his pocket.

✭ ✩ ✱ ✦

The post office is

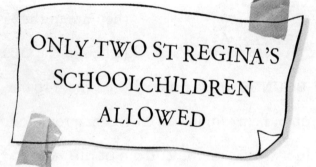

ONLY TWO ST REGINA'S
SCHOOLCHILDREN
ALLOWED

but it is okay because Georgia May is not

at St Regina's, she is at The Drabble Academy

for Girls, so when we go in Mrs. Butterworth

cannot say a thing except for,

And I say, "No but my gran does," which is almost true because only just now I said, "Goodbye, Gran, we are going to the shops to cut hair for money." And she said, "Super." Although I am not sure if it was to me or because a hamster had just not died **MIRACULOUSLY** on telly, but I did not decide to find out, so off we went.

Mrs. Butterworth does not ask if Cosmo's mum knows where he is because Cosmo's mum is always saying how she believes in **FREEDOM** and **SELF-EXPRESSION**, i.e. Cosmo is allowed to do what he likes so he can learn to be **RESPONSIBLE** etc. You can tell Mrs. Butterworth does not believe in **FREEDOM** or **SELF EXPRESSION**, but she does believe in

haircuts because what she does say is, "It is about time you had your hair cut — it was hard to tell if you were a boy or a girl, Cosmo Moon Webster." Cosmo says "I have other evidence" but Mrs. Butterworth does not want to see the other evidence. Nor does she want to lend us scissors in exchange for cutting her moustache, which she says is not a moustache at all and she will be reporting me to my mum for saying it is.

So then we do not have any scissors and I am already in trouble and we have spent our collateral on liquorice sticks and are chewing them on the wall outside, when we see Bridget Grimes riding her bike on the pavement. She says,

What are you doing loitering, Penelope Jones?

And I say, "We are not loitering we are
hairdressing, only we don't have any
scissors — can we borrow some and
cut your hair, it is only £5?" She says,
"Absolutely not and I would not do
that if I were you, Penelope Jones."

Which is what she is always saying because she is top of the class and our headmaster Mr. Schumann's favourite. But luckily Georgia May Morton-Jones says, "You *shouldn't be riding on the pavement, Bridget Grimes, it is against the law and you will be arrested and put in prison.*" And Bridget Grimes shuts up, and I am glad that Georgia May Morton-Jones came after all because sometimes knowing a lot of rules is useful.

But we still don't have any scissors and then Cosmo sees Brady O'Grady coming out of the butcher's with Mrs. O'Grady (who has a tattoo of a heart and a dagger on her arm) and it is **OBVIOUS** that he has quite recently had all his hair shaved off, even the cross which was there

before, and so it won't need doing again for
three days yet. But this gives me another

BRILLIANT IDEA™,

which is that, even though we do not have
scissors, Dad has an electric razor and I am not
even banned from using it yet. So we go all the
way back home again.

★ ☆ ✦ ✱

The razor is amazing. It is called the Silent
Strimmer and has three lengths and two speeds,
i.e. *fast* and *super fast*. On the advert it says
THE CLOSEST SHAVE and I know it is true
because Aunt Deedee wrote the advert.

Cosmo says, "Have you ever used it
before?" And I say, "No but I have watched

Dad about a gazillion times and it cannot be that hard because Dad is not good at machines, e.g. the DVD player which he still does not know how to use after two years." But Cosmo says we should test it first so we decide to do Barry because he can't complain and also he is very hairy. Cosmo says he will be in charge of the Strimmer because he is a week older and also a boy and boys are better at machines, but I remind him about **a)** Dad and the DVD player,

32

b) that Sunflower is always telling him off for saying stuff like that, and **3)** that it is more my razor than his so I will do it.

But I am soon regretting it because when I shave the top of Barry's head he scratches me on the nose and I am mortally wounded.

Cosmo says it would not have happened if he was in charge and that I am too injured to go on, but I say it is fine, I am like *Animal SOS* and will **MIRACULOUSLY NOT DIE**. But I decide that I have done enough of Barry (plus he has hidden himself inside the dishwasher and I am not allowed to touch the dishwasher for a lot of reasons) so we should do Gran instead.

Except that when we go into the living room Gran is fast asleep. Cosmo says we should wake her up or the Strimmer will scare her but I say it is fine as Gran will sleep through anything, even an earthquake according to Mum, which is true because when I accidentally blew up the cooker everyone came running downstairs and Daisy was crying in case it was terrorists, but Gran did not move even a muscle. Plus the Silent Strimmer is not noisy or we will get our money back, according to Aunt Deedee's advert.

And Cosmo is amazed because Gran really does not wake up even when she is bald and looks like her friend Arthur Peason. And we are all totally pleased except that then I remember that I have only done one haircut which is not enough to pay Mum back for the India phone call and we need to find someone else. So we are racking our heads trying to think of people, but all we can think of is Me, except I do not have any money.

And then I notice that Georgia May Morton-Jones is not racking her head at all, she is not even in the living room. And then I am worried that a **CATASTROPHE** has happened, i.e. she has been kidnapped by international gangsters. But Cosmo says that **STATISTICALLY** you are more likely to be killed by a donkey than get kidnapped by international gangsters. And he is half right because she has not been kidnapped or killed by a donkey, she is in the kitchen and so is the

Silent Strimmer and she has
silently strimmed her head
and is now as bald as Gran
and Arthur Peason.

Cosmo says that it is
actually brilliant because
now Aunt Deedee can
give me £5 and I
will have made
my fortune,
but I am
not entirely and
completely sure because Aunt Deedee is always
banging on about how Georgia May Morton-
Jones's hair is the envy of The Drabble
Academy for Girls because of how it is so curly.

And then Georgia May Morton-Jones starts to cry because Barry is chewing the hair on the floor. So then I have my last

BRILLIANT IDEA™,

which is to glue the hair back on to Georgia May Morton-Jones's head.

Only when we have finished, Georgia May Morton-Jones's head does not look like it did before the Silent Strimmer. It is quite a lot of different lengths and there is a big bare bit on the top where we ran out of hair because Barry ate some, plus some more blew into the garden. And Georgia May starts to cry again and that is when Gran wakes up and Daisy comes downstairs and Mum and Dad come home

all at once which Cosmo says is a **CONSPIRACY**, but it is not, it is a **COINCIDENCE**, and they are not the same – I have checked with Mr. Schumann.

Anyway, a lot of things happen then, which are:

1. Mum goes a bit pale.

b. Gran sees herself in the mirror and thinks all her hair has fallen out like Arthur Peason's and Dad has to give her a rum and blackcurrant to calm down.

3. Barry does a chokey noise because he has got some of Georgia May's hair stuck in his throat so Dad has to pull it out like on *Animal SOS* and so Barry **MIRACULOUSLY DOES NOT DIE.**

Then Mum says, "Oh lawks, what are we going to tell Aunt Deedee?" And I say, "Well you can tell her it **WASN'T** me, because I only did the glueing bit." And Dad calls me Penny Dreadful and does the honking goose laugh and Mum goes even more pale and says, "If you cannot say something helpful, Gordon, then don't say anything at all." Then Cosmo says, "I have got something helpful to say, i.e. we can glue a hat on the hair so Aunt Deedee won't see the bald patch." And Dad says that is not a bad idea but Mum is not so sure and tells Cosmo it is high time he went home.

But then Mum doesn't have any better ideas so she finds my old policeman's helmet to put on Georgia May Morton-Jones, only Georgia May has been lying on the floor doing her sobbing and has superglued her head to the carpet. So Cosmo says it is either the hair or the carpet that must be chopped off and sacrificed, because he is very keen on sacrifices. Mum says, "I thought I told you to go home, Cosmo Moon Webster." But in the end she decides it is the hair to be sacrificed, so she gets the Silent Strimmer and shaves Georgia May **AGAIN**.

And that is when
Aunt Deedee walks in.

At first Aunt Deedee **DOES NOT SAY A WORD**.

Which is when Dad has a

BRILLIANT IDEA™

i.e. to get the hoover to suck up the clippings,

so me and Cosmo and Daisy and Gran all whizz

out with him in case it is very heavy and also

because of him being not very good at machinery.

And then we do not have to listen to Aunt

Deedee doing the shouting, which is mostly

about how Georgia May will not be allowed to

be a princess in The Drabble Academy for Girls

Ballet Recital because they all have to have

regulation buns and she will have to be a bee

and wear a furry helmet like Phoebe Patterson-

Parry who everyone knows has two left feet.

Which Cosmo said would be a brilliant way to make money, having two left feet, because you would be a phenomenon and people would pay to look at them. And Dad says, "Did I ever tell you I could have been a ballet dancer if I hadn't met your mother?" And then he does a pirouette and knocks over a bottle of Dandelion and Burdock, which is when Cosmo decides it is time to go home after all.

And I am now doubly gloomy because no one paid me for the haircuts, not even Gran because she says no one will sit next to her at bingo except Arthur Peason. Plus Mum says now I owe Dad £19.99 because the Silent Strimmer is not at all silent any more and it cannot strim either, mainly because it is clogged with superglue.

And Aunt Deedee says no, Dad cannot get his money back because it is **USER ERROR**. So I am not allowed to go to Monkey Madness tomorrow after all.

Daisy says, "*It is all your own fault, Penelope Jones, you are such a complete* **MORON**." But it is not my fault. I am just a

Magnet for Disaster.

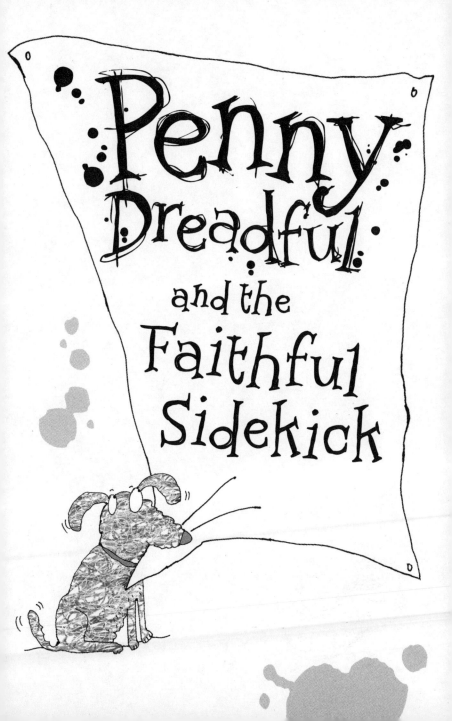

The dog was not
my fault **AT ALL**.
In fact if it is anyone's fault it
is Gran's because she
watches too much
Animal SOS, which
is a TV series
where animals
are always
nearly dying but
then they don't and it is
MIRACULOUS, which is
where me and Cosmo got
the idea in the first place.

53

✦ ✧ ✦ ✦

What happened was, we were watching this
episode where they found this huge and hairy
Alsatian which was **COMPLETELY** abandoned
and thin and very sad, and also had a cut
on its paw. And after it **MIRACULOUSLY DID**

NOT DIE a policeman
took it home and
called it Alan
and trained it
to be his faithful
sidekick and
sniff out
burglars
and all sorts.

And then I had my first

BRILLIANT IDEA™,

which was to
have our own
faithful sidekick
because then
we could train
it to sniff out
criminals or treasure
or at least the chocolate
biscuit that I lost last
Wednesday and which

MYSTERIOUSLY

DISAPPEARED very

near Gran's cat Barry.

Sniff Sniff

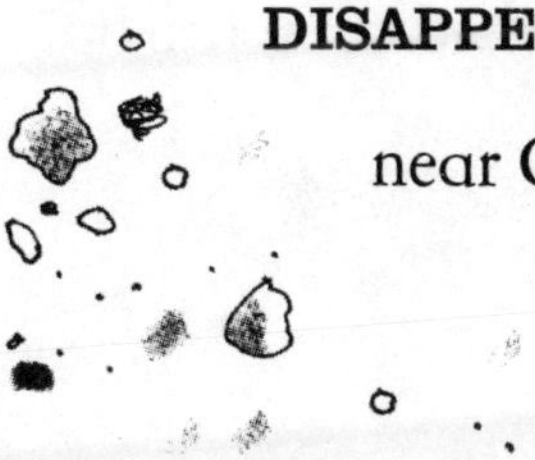

Except that Mum says the only mystery is that Barry is not completely huge and having to be wheeled around on a cart what with all the cereal and biscuits and other **NOT CAT BISCUIT** things that he eats. So then I asked Mum if we could get an Alsatian, only not called Alan, called Killer or Rex, but she said Alsatians are pedigree dogs and cost hundreds of pounds and I still owe her for the India phone call and the Silent Strimmer thing so no I cannot have one. And Cosmo can't have one because his mum Sunflower is a cat person. Although they do not have a cat either in case the cat kills other animals, which Sunflower is very much against, especially when they are on the kitchen floor in bits.

So then we are totally
FLUMMOXED, which
is a long word in our
spelling bee this week and
means **CONFUSED**,
according to
Miss Patterson
our teacher who is
very tall and thin like
a beanpole and who said,
e.g., "Penelope Jones,
I am completely
FLUMMOXED as to
why you have spelled
'Orangutan' with a Q."
Only it wasn't a "Q"

it was an "O", but my pen slipped because Henry Potts threw a rubber at Cosmo but it hit me by mistake.

But then Gran said in fact cats are very good sidekicks, e.g. Barry, e.g. he does not like the man who does the news who looks a bit strange and prefers the nice weather lady with the long hair so obviously he is a good judge of character. So I said we could train Barry just like Alan if we tied a lead onto his collar, only we didn't have a lead so we used Cosmo's belt which possibly would have been excellent except for:

a) Barry did not very much want to be on a lead and bit my hand and it is **MIRACULOUS** I did not die because his teeth are very pointy.

b) The only thing Barry could sniff out were cornflakes and he got cross when we did not let him have any because Mum says it is

CAT BISCUITS AND CAT BISCUITS ONLY, and so he went back to watching the racing on telly with Gran.

3. Cosmo's trousers kept falling down and he tripped over Dad's binoculars (which I had borrowed to see if I could look into Mrs. Nugent over-the-road's living room because Gran wants to know if she really has got a plasma telly or if it is a lie) and knocked his head on the table, which wobbled and a glass of orange squash fell off and landed on Barry, who is very hairy and hard to clean.

So then, **d)** Mum said,

> I have had quite enough hoohah today what with Daisy and Lucy B. Finnegan who are upstairs trying to be pop stars, and can you please go out and leave me in peace for five minutes, thank you.

So we did.

So in fact it might be Mum's fault, because
if she hadn't made us go out, we would never
have found Rex in the first place.

What happened was that we decided to
go to the post office because there is a pound
coin stuck to the concrete outside and it is
quite fun to watch people try to pick it up,
only when we got to the shops the pound
coin was gone and a dog was there instead,
only not stuck to the concrete, just sitting
on it eating a stick.

And I said,

That dog is quite thinnish and sad and is possibly **ABANDONED** and we should rescue him and train him to be our faithful sidekick, because if we don't he will have to have a lethal injection and he won't even get to heaven because I have checked and Mr. Schumann said dogs do not get in.

And Cosmo said, "I have seen that dog before, I am not sure he is completely abandoned and maybe we should ask Mrs. Butterworth," who is the lady who runs the post office and has a moustache and who I am not very keen on because she is always saying stuff like "I have got my beady eye on you" and it is very beady, but Cosmo said we had to. Only when we went in Mrs. Butterworth said, "Cosmo Moon Webster and Penelope Jones, go out immediately — it is **ONLY TWO ST REGINA'S SCHOOLCHILDREN ALLOWED**, can you not read?" And I said, "Yes we can read but we cannot see through walls and so we did not know that Cherry Scarpelli and Bridget Grimes were already in here buying crisps, which in fact are bad for you and you might get clogged and die and end up in heaven but your dog won't." And Mrs. Butterworth said she would be reporting me to my mum for answering back, so you see you cannot win with her and her beady eye.

And then when we got outside the dog

stood up and started jumping up and down a lot so I said it must definitely be abandoned and is trying to tell us to take it home and train it to catch criminals. And Cosmo said, "It is not an Alsatian, it is very small and maybe it is not the right sort of dog." But I said, "It is probably just a puppy and look he has just sniffed that I have got some spilled yoghurt on my trousers so he is obviously **SUPERIORLY INTELLIGENT**."

Which is what the policeman said Alan was. So then Cosmo said, "Fine but I get to have the lead because I am older and a dog person." And I said no because I have a Dogs of the World poster and have watched *One Hundred and One Dalmatians* so I know all about dogs. So then Cosmo said he would give me 10p if he could have the lead first and I said yes as long as we call him Rex.

And Rex was very happy with this arrangement because he did not bite us or dig his claws in like Barry, he just walked happily next to Cosmo and tried to eat lots of stuff like crisp packets and a lamp post.

And I said Mum would be very pleased because we had saved her hundreds of pounds in Alsatian money and Dad would be very pleased because he is always saying how he could have been a police dog handler if he hadn't met Mum.

Only when we got home Mum did not seem very pleased at all, in fact her voice went all squeaky and high like it does sometimes and Dad says only dogs and dolphins can understand it. Only Rex did not seem to understand it when she said, "Penelope Jones, what the blazes have you done this time? You get that dog out of here this instant and take it right back where it came from," because he just carried on chewing one of Dad's trainers. And I said, "I can't take him back because he is COMPLETELY ABANDONED and

they will give him a lethal injection and he won't even get into heaven," and Gran said, "It is true they do not let dogs into heaven — Arthur Peason was dead for one whole minute when he had his operation and the man on the gates told him his spaniel Maurice couldn't come in and that is the only reason Arthur is alive today."

And Mum said, "I do not have time for this, I have to be at the surgery in five minutes but I do not want to see that dog when I get home." And I said she wouldn't, he would be **MIRACULOUSLY ELSEWHERE**, i.e. at Cosmo's possibly.

Only when she had gone Cosmo reminded me that Sunflower is a cat person and that she is not keen on dogs because they are not very intelligent and have a bad aura. And I said Rex was in fact **SUPERIORLY INTELLIGENT** except he wasn't showing it at that exact moment because he was too busy trying to get into the washing machine, unless he was trying to say he needed a bath in which case he was doubly clever.

But Cosmo still said no and so did Lucy B.
Finnegan because she already has a parakeet
and gerbils, and Daisy said,

You are a **MORON** if you think anyone is going to want that hairy thing, Penelope Jones.

And then they went back upstairs
to be pop stars again.

So that is when I had my

BRILLIANT IDEA™

number two, which was that Aunt Deedee
is a dog person and she had to send her dog
Llewellyn back to the dog shop because he
kept yapping at Georgia May Morton-Jones
(i.e. my cousin) and her fingers are very
important because Mr. Nakamura says she
shows potential on the violin. And I said Rex
is not at all yappy and he is just the sort of
dog that Aunt Deedee might like and it will
make her less cross with me after the Silent
Strimmer thing so it is definitely a

BRILLIANT IDEA™

★ ☆ ✦ ✦

So me and Cosmo took Rex round to Aunt
Deedee's house, which is only four roads away
but it is very much bigger than ours and also
much cleaner because of all the rules, e.g.:

1. No eating except at the table.

2. No plasticine or paint or glue except
at the table and only if it is covered in a
plastic cloth.

C. No eating plasticine or paint or glue.

Plus if you even **LOOK** at a glass candlestick
she says, "Do not even think about it,
Penelope Jones." Only when we got there
Aunt Deedee was at work, i.e. at a **CRUNCH**

MEETING WITH THE NEW YORK BOYS, and Georgia May Morton-Jones was being looked after by the new au pair who is called Lilya Bobylev and is from Russia (which is where all au pairs come from) and has not been sacked yet for **NOT MEASURING UP** although Gran says it is only a matter of time.

So I said,

Hello, Lilya Bobylev, this is Rex, he is for Aunt Deedee. She definitely wants him because he is not yappy and will not eat Georgia May's fingers so she can play violin.

And Lilya said,

I do not think Mrs. Morton-Jones very happy with dog.

And I said,

Yes she is, she is a dog person and you have to keep him because of the hair shaving.

And then there was a crash from the dining room because Georgia May had accidentally poked a glass candlestick with her violin bow, so Lilya had to go and glue it back together (but only at the table with the cloth), so we just went in.

Georgia May did not seem very pleased with Rex either at first because of her violin fingers, but then Cosmo showed her he is not at all yappy and then he put his head in Rex's mouth like a lion, only he did not leave it there long because he said it smelled of meat and he is vegetarian.

So then Georgia May seemed a bit happier and said we could dress Rex up in her tutu and her furry bee helmet (that she had to wear at ballet because of not having a regulation bun) because he would be much prettier that way.

And she was right, Rex did look much prettier in a tutu and a bee helmet, only he did not want to dance to her Children's Introduction to Mozart CD,

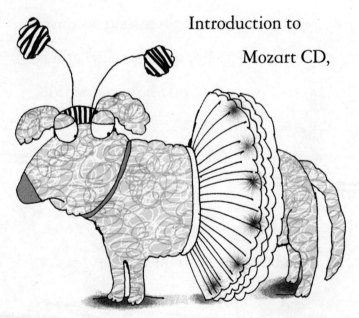

he wanted to swallow things. In fact quite a
lot of things, i.e.:

1. Four digestive biscuits

b. A banana

c) The key to the back door

4. And the speaking end of

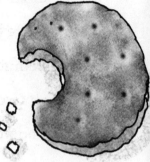

Georgia May Morton-Jones's
baby monitor, which Aunt Deedee
still uses because she can make
sure Georgia May is doing her
violin practice and also issue
instructions down it to Lilya.

✷ ✩ ✫ ✭

Lilya said, "This not good at all,
Mrs. Morton-Jones not happy,"
and Cosmo said "She *is* never happy,

so eating the key and the monitor won't
make much difference." Which is true. But
Lilya did not agree and said we had to take
the bee helmet and tutu off Rex and then go
home and Georgia May had to go to her
room and do Mandarin practice (which is not
about being an orange, it is another language,
like Chinese). So Georgia May went upstairs
and then an amazing thing happened
because suddenly we could hear her saying
"*Wo Jiao Georgia May Morton-Jones*",
only it did not come out of her mouth it
came right out of Rex. And Cosmo said,
"It is the other end bit of the baby
monitor." And he went upstairs and got
the speaker bit and showed us by saying

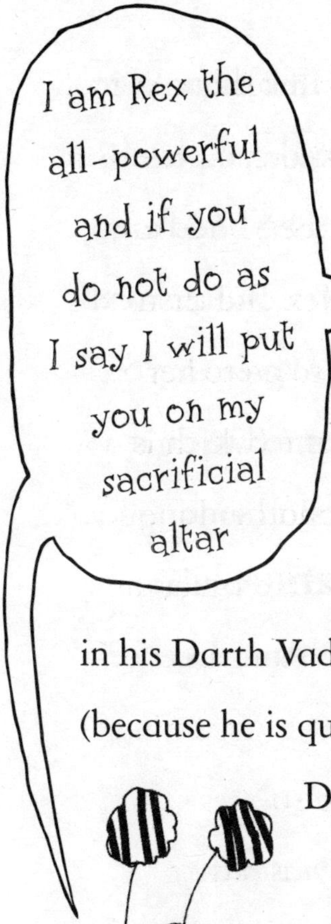

I am Rex the all-powerful and if you do not do as I say I will put you on my sacrificial altar

in his Darth Vadar voice

(because he is quite keen on

Darth Vadar

and sacrificial altars)

and it was brilliant

because the voice

came right

out of Rex.

Although I am not sure that Rex thought it was brilliant – in fact he looked completely **FLUMMOXED**. But anyway then I had a go and I made Rex sound like Mrs. Butterworth by saying "*I have my beady eye on you*" a lot. And then even Lilya wanted to do it and she made Rex sing a Russian song, which was doubly **FLUMMOXING** and not just for Rex. And that is when Aunt Deedee walked in.

At first Aunt Deedee was also **FLUMMOXED** because there was a dog singing in Russian in her living room dressed in a tutu and a furry bee helmet, but then she saw me and Cosmo and she said a lot of things starting with how I am a complete

and utter nuisance and
which end up with her
sacking Lilya and
calling Mum.

★ ★ ★ ★

Mum was not at all happy about coming because she had only just got in from work and Daisy was crying because Lucy B. Finnegan said she was not at all in tune, so Mum made Dad come too, who was also not happy about coming because Barry had rubbed against his leg and it was all sticky from the spilled squash.

When they got here Aunt Deedee showed them the baby monitor thing by talking into it and saying,

I have had it up to here with your daughter, she is a **BAD INFLUENCE**. This cost £49.99.

Only of course Rex said it, which was actually

very scary.

And Cosmo said, "It will be okay because
Rex will just poo it out in a day or so
and then you can have it back," but Aunt
Deedee did not want the monitor back and Rex
said so. And then Mum said, "I told you I
wanted that dog out of my sight," and
I said, "He was out of your sight only you
came round here, so it is not my fault,
it is yours," and Dad said, "Penny Dreadful!"
and did the honking goose laugh, only Mum
gave him one of her looks so he turned it into
a cough and said,

Where did you get the
dog from anyway?

And Cosmo said outside the post office, and
I said how Rex was completely **ABANDONED**
and about to have a lethal injection and not
get into heaven etc., but Dad said, "No he
wasn't, he has a tag on his collar,
look." And we did look and he was
right and the tag said,

My name is
Clarence
– if I am lost
please return me
to Mrs. Higgins
at 19 Newton
Street

And Cosmo
said, "Oh that
is where I have seen him before," because
Cosmo lives at 21 Newton Street, i.e. next door,

and Mum gave Cosmo one of her looks and he decided it was time to go home. And I said Clarence was not a good name for a faithful sidekick, he should be Rex or Killer, and Mum gave me one of her looks so I decided it was time to go home too. Only Dad said I couldn't, I had to go with him to take Clarence back to Mrs. Higgins, so in the end me and Cosmo both went while Mum paid for the baby monitor and tried to unsack Lilya.

★ ☆ ✦ ✷

Mrs. Higgins was completely pleased to see Clarence and said she had only left him outside the post office while she went in for a stamp and when she came out he had **VANISHED INTO THIN AIR** and where on earth did we find him?

Dad said he was on
Hollyhock Road,
which is
not a
complete
lie because
that is
where
Aunt
Deedee
lives
and
anyway it
is for the
**GREATER
GOOD**.

And Mrs. Higgins said, "Oh thank you, I was so worried because he is on a special diet and if you are not careful he will eat anything. He has not eaten anything, has he?" And Dad said no, which was another lie but was also for the **GREATER GOOD**, or at least he says it will be as long as Rex does not go near Aunt Deedee's house and the other end of the baby monitor for a while, because that could be quite shocking for Mrs. Higgins.

★ ☆ ✹ ✸

So now we are not allowed **EVER** to get a faithful sidekick because Mum says I have proved I am **NOT RESPONSIBLE** with animals, plus now I owe her for the baby monitor as well and will be paying her back **UNTIL KINGDOM COME**, so I asked her when Kingdom would come but she gave me another one of her looks, so I shut up then.

Daisy said, "*It is all your own fault, Penelope Jones, you are such a complete* **MORON**." But it is not my fault. I am just a

Magnet for Disaster.

Penny Dreadful
and the School Inspector

Mr. Schumann is our headmaster

and he mostly says things like "Penelope Jones, I am **SICK AND TIRED** of seeing you on the naughty chair", which is not actually a chair that has been naughty, it is a chair for naughty people which is outside his office, and it is true I am quite often on it even though I am not actually naughty, I am just a **MAGNET FOR DISASTER**.

Anyway he has been **SICK AND TIRED** even more than usual because a School Inspector is coming to St Regina's to check that it is **UP TO SCRATCH**,

otherwise it will be shut down and we will all have to troop to Chipping Broadley Non-Denominational Middle School on the bus, which I said sounded actually quite brilliant but Bridget Grimes (who is top of the class and Mr. Schumann's favourite) said her mum said Mrs. Butterworth in the post office said that the Burton twins go there and they have ringworm and drink ketchup, plus the bus smells of sick since the trip to Mole Hall Wildlife Park, so we are better off at St Regina's. Although I have seen Cosmo drink ketchup and he has had nits three times this year, so it is just the smelly bus really.

So on Thursday Mr. Schumann comes into our classroom at circle time (which is when we are supposed to be all sitting on the floor talking about Henry VIII and other interesting things, except that I am in the corner with Cosmo because we have had an argument with Bridget Grimes about otters) and he tells Miss Patterson (who is our teacher and who is very tall and thin like a beanpole)

that we have to be on our best behaviour and
there is to be absolutely **NO NONSENSE OR
SHENANIGANS** whatsoever and if there is then
whoever does the shenanigans will be in **BIG
TROUBLE**. And when he says that he looks me
right in the eye, which is not completely fair
because I have only been in **BIG TROUBLE** four
times this term:

1. For sticking a gel pen up Bridget Grimes's nose to see if it would reach her brain, which it did not, but it is not because she does not have one, which is what Cosmo said, it is because noses are not made for pens, according to Miss Patterson.

2. For bringing Barry to school in my bag for show-and-tell, although in fact he was the most interesting show-and-tell **EVER** because

he ran up the curtain in the dinner hall and got stuck and the fire brigade

had to come and rescue
him and we all got to
go on the fire truck,
so if you think about it
I should get a gold star.

C. For telling Mr. Schumann that Gran was
dead and that I would not be able to do my
maths homework because I had to sit by her
grave and weep.

4. For proving that the most biscuits you
can eat before you are sick is twenty-three
which is actually quite scientific
so in fact I should get
another gold star.

Anyway, then he says the Inspector is coming at nine o'clock tomorrow so we have twenty-four hours to **SHARPEN UP OUR ACT**, which means absolutely no throwing rubbers at people and absolutely lots of maths. Cosmo says actually it is only nineteen hours because it is two o'clock already and maybe Mr. Schumann should absolutely do lots of maths too, but Mr. Schumann does not look like he wants to do maths, he looks like he wants to throw a rubber at Cosmo but luckily he can't because that would be **SHENANIGANS**.

Mr. Schumann also says it is **STRICTLY UNIFORM ONLY** tomorrow, i.e. red top, grey bottoms, white socks and black shoes, and he looks at me again at that bit, because I am not

wearing a red top I am wearing a green one
(which is not entirely my fault, it is because
I was showing Daisy how it is possible to drink
Sugar Pops out of the bowl upside down, only it
turns out it is not possible and they just fall all
over you), and also at Cosmo, because Cosmo
is wearing a Jedi outfit and wellies.

⭐ ⭐ ⭐ ⭐

So next morning I make sure I am almost completely wearing **STRICTLY UNIFORM ONLY**, i.e. my red top because Mum has got most of the Sugar Pops out with a sponge, and it is only my socks which are not **STRICT** because yesterday's white ones have got holes in them from where I showed Cosmo how to make a glove puppet and the only ones left are stripey, but at least it is red and white stripes so it is half **STRICT**.

But when I meet Cosmo at the end of Newton Street he is **NOT IN UNIFORM AT ALL**. This is because Sunflower, his mum, who is actually called Barbara, does not believe in uniform because it is oppressive and made of polyester, she believes in **FREEDOM** and **SELF-EXPRESSION** and also in natural fibres, so Cosmo is wearing a long cloak and flip-flops.

I say Mr. Schumann will not be happy, in fact he will be **SICK AND TIRED**, but Cosmo says he has an official letter from Sunflower saying it is against the law to make him wear uniform until he is eleven and she will stage a one-woman sit-in protest outside Mr. Schumann's office if he tries to send Cosmo home.

Which is exactly what Mr. Schumann tries to do when Cosmo walks into school, only Cosmo shows him the official letter and

Mr. Schumann decides he does not want Sunflower sitting outside his office protesting when the School Inspector is here, so he says Cosmo will just have to say it is religious grounds.

Then he tells Miss Patterson to put me and Cosmo at the back of class where we are almost hidden by Alexander Pringle, who wears age 14 clothes even though he is nine because of his glands and also because he is always eating, and so the School Inspector will possibly not see that Cosmo is wearing the cloak.

But when Mr. Schumann is gone back to his office to do waiting, Bridget Grimes puts her hand up and says,

But Miss Patterson, Miss, if they are at the back then they will whisper and throw things which is **SHENANIGANS**.

and Miss Patterson decides that Bridget Grimes

is right and she makes us swap with Luke Bruce

and Brady O'Grady who are more in the middle.

Only then Cosmo is utterly visible and plus also

he is right next to Henry Potts who is his mortal enemy, and almost immediately Cosmo has to throw a rubber at him and it misses and hits a jar of blue paint, which goes all over Bridget Grimes's grey bottoms so she has to get changed into her PE shorts,

which are not grey
at all but are purple
and have butterflies
on them. So then Miss
Patterson decides we should
go back to where Mr. Schumann put us,
so we have to swap again with Luke Bruce
and Brady O'Grady and sit next to the locust
tank, which is good because you can watch
them scuttling around and jumping like
grasshoppers through the special shatterproof
glass. Except that Miss Patterson says there is
to be absolutely no staring at the locusts and
instead we have to stare at the whiteboard
and concentrate on the lots of maths because
the School Inspector will be here **ANY MINUTE**.

But he is not here **ANY MINUTE** because after about a whole hour I notice out of the corner of my eye (which is mostly staring at the whiteboard) that Mr. Schumann is standing at the gate looking up and down the road and he is almost definitely **SICK AND TIRED**. And by this point everyone is getting a bit **SICK AND TIRED** of all the maths and even Bridget Grimes has got two answers wrong which is a **MIRACLE** and so she is crying

and Luke Bruce
is asleep

and Alexander
Pringle is eating
a jam sandwich.

So Miss Patterson decides that we have possibly done enough maths even for Mr. Schumann and that maybe we should do some art instead because it is important to show that we are creative as well as knowing how many nines make forty-five, but that we cannot use the paint as there has already been one accident so we will do collages instead.

And so we get the scissors and glue and cardboard and glittery bits out and me and Cosmo decide we are going to do a collage of aliens invading Planet Earth, and then everyone is cutting and glueing like **MAD**, only then Cosmo notices that

he has accidentally glued his cloak to the desk
and so Miss Patterson makes him take it off
and underneath is the Jedi outfit, and I can tell

Miss Patterson is

beginning to

be **SICK**

AND

TIRED

too.

Especially because then Brady O'Grady tips all the glittery bits over his head because he says he is part of his own collage, which under normal circumstances Miss Patterson would say is actually quite **CREATIVE** but today she just says, *"I think that is quite enough art for today and maybe we should do our topic of Ancient Egypt because they did not have glue or glitter there."*

We are going to try to build pyramids out of the wooden blocks like slaves, which is maths and creativity at once, and Mr. Schumann will be totally **NOT SICK AND TIRED**.

And Miss Patterson says me and Cosmo can work with Bridget Grimes and Cherry Scarpelli because they will cancel us out with their brains. But actually she is wrong because it turns out that me and Cosmo are totally brilliant at pyramids and we build our side super-fast and Bridget Grimes gets cross and says, "Miss Patterson, Penelope Jones and Cosmo Moon Webster have hogged all the blocks and I have not got a single one." So then Henry Potts throws a block at Bridget Grimes but it misses

and hits me on the nose.

So I throw it back at Henry only it misses
him and hits the locust tank, which it
turns out is not shatterproof
after all and it breaks and
all the locusts fly out.

And that is when Mr. Schumann and the
School Inspector walk in.

And everyone goes very quiet, except
Bridget Grimes who is crying because there
are several locusts stuck in her hair,

and also the locusts are not completely quiet,
they are quite buzzy. And Mr. Schumann is
looking right at me, even though he cannot
know it is me who threw the block at the

locust tank unless he has X-ray eyes, which are
not real they are only in films, so I say,

Actually it is totally on purpose,
Mr. Schumann, because we are being
Ancient Egyptians and there were a
lot of locusts in Ancient Egypt.

And Cosmo says,

Yes there was
a complete
plague of
them and
they devoured
everything in
their path.

Then Bridget Grimes cries even more because
she says the locusts are going to devour her.
Only Alexander Pringle says if she does not be
quiet *he* will devour her and he once ate four
helpings of sponge pudding at lunch so Bridget
shuts up quite quickly. And then Miss Patterson
decides it is time we did PE and so she sends
everyone out to change into their shorts, except
Bridget who is already in hers, and Cosmo, who
says he has an official letter not to do PE because
it is too **COMPETITIVE AND AGGRESSIVE**,
and me, because she says I have to go and sit on
the naughty chair and wait for Mr. Schumann
to punish me. And the whole time Mr. Schumann
is looking completely **SICK AND TIRED** and the
Inspector is writing like **MAD** in his notebook

and I think he is definitely writing down that

St Regina's has to be closed because of the

NOT AT ALL STRICT UNIFORM and the

fighting and the escaped locusts

(which have noticed the door and are all heading out

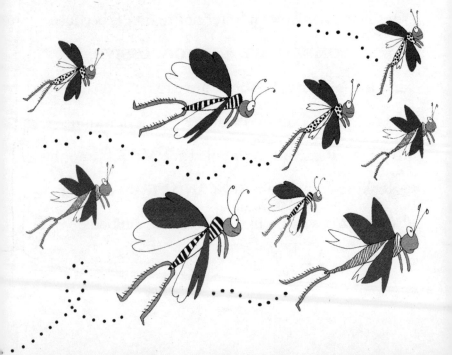

of it in a *giant* swarm).

And then it gets worse when I am sitting
on the chair, because the School Inspector
comes and sits on another not-naughty chair
next to me and asks me a lot of questions
about the chair, i.e. *how many times
have you had to sit on the naughty
chair? What sort of things have you
been sent to sit on the chair for?
How many lessons have you
missed to sit on the chair?*
And Mr. Schumann is standing
behind him staring me right in
the eye, so I absolutely **DO NOT
LIE** and I say I have sat on it at
least twenty-seven times this
year, mostly for throwing stuff,

and I have missed maths several times and
the trip to the museum to see the stuffed lion
and the roman coins.

Headmaster's
Office

And I am thinking that even if St Regina's is not closed down then I am going to be in **BIG TROUBLE** again and possibly even excluded for ever.

And when I get home I have to tell Mum and Dad what has happened and Daisy says,

It is all your own fault, Penelope Jones, you are such a **MORON**!

even though it is **OBVIOUS** that it is Henry Potts's fault because he threw the block first, or possibly Bridget's fault for saying she didn't have a block. And anyway Daisy should be sad because now I am going to have to troop on the bus to Chipping Broadley Non-Denominational Middle School with the Burton Twins and probably get ringworm and have to drink ketchup.

Only Daisy says in fact I can be home-schooled like Fraser Forks, who gets to make rhubarb crumble and read about whales all day and it is unfair and why can't we both be home-schooled? And Mum says **NO ONE** is being home-schooled because she would rather try to teach Barry to knit, and to please stop all the nonsense.

✦ ✧ ✦ ✦

Only a very **UNUSUAL** thing happens when I

go into school on Monday. Which is that the

school is not shut down and I am not sent to

Chipping Broadley Non-Denominational

Middle School to drink ketchup and catch

ringworm, or home to make rhubarb crumble

and read about whales. But there is a very big

change, apart from the locusts, which Miss

Patterson says were last seen heading towards

Chipping Broadley, and that is that the

naughty chair

is completely

VANISHED

And when I ask Mr. Schumann where it is he says it is in the cupboard because apparently it is not very **PROGRESSIVE** to have a naughty chair and miss trips to museums. So in fact it is entirely my fault.

And for once I do not argue.

Penny Dreadful's Top 5 Tips for Survival

Sometimes it is very **ARDUOUS** being a

MAGNET FOR DISASTER. Especially if

you are extra specially magnetic, i.e. like me.

But even though it is **ARDUOUS**, it is also

very **INFORMATIVE**,

i.e. I have learned

some important

TOP TIPS

about how to

avoid complete

CATASTROPHE.

Number 1

Get a DISGUISE

It is completely
important not to
look like me, i.e.
Penelope Jones,
when I am being
very magnetic,
e.g. accidentally
knocking over a teetering pile of envelopes
in the post office. So sometimes I dress up as
Cosmo, i.e. in a Jedi outfit and wellies, because
it completely confuses Mrs. Butterworth's
beady eye and however hard she **RACKS**
her brain she is **FLUMMOXED** as to who to
shout at.

Another good
disguise is dressing up
as a burglar, because
burglars wear balaclavas
which **COMPLETELY**
cover up their face.

Although it is possible you would get shouted at
for being a burglar anyway.

Number 2
Collect COLLATERAL, i.e. money

Coins are **EVERYWHERE**, e.g. on the ground
outside the post office,
down the back of the
sofa and mostly in
Dad's trouser pocket.

Collect them **ALL** because you never know

when you might need them for:

1. Paying people back, e.g. your Aunt Deedee

when you have accidentally broken a glass

vase or phoned Russia for instance.

b) Buying essential supplies

like biscuits or liquorice sticks.

iii. Playing ludo, because you have

used the actual plastic counters to

flick at your mortal enemy.

Number 3
Be PREPARED for EVERY EVENTUALITY

DISASTERS are EVERYWHERE and you never

know when you might be super-magnetic,

so it is completely important to have a box
of useful things for **EVERY EVENTUALITY**,
i.e. anything, e.g.:

a) **COLLATERAL** (see above).

2. **A DISGUISE** (see above).

3. Biscuits (for **ARDUOUS
JOURNEYS**).

4. A bottle of washing-up liquid and a
sponge (for when you have spilled something,
or accidentally drawn some Roman soldiers
marching along the kitchen wall).

e) A torch, for when you have accidentally
blown up the hoover by trying to suck up the
washing-up liquid, and all the lights have
gone off.

Number 4
Find a TRUSTY SCAPEGOAT

This means someone else to **BLAME**, e.g. in our house everyone mostly blames me, even though it is not usually my fault, it is that I am a **MAGNET FOR DISASTER**. So I usually blame Barry the cat, because he is most often eating things that are **NOT** cat biscuits. E.g. when Daisy said, "Where is my last cherry chocolate, Penelope Jones? I **KNOW** it is you who has eaten it," I said, "But in fact perhaps it is not I, it is **BARRY**, because he is completely **KEEN** on cherries and chocolate, so ha!"

Number 5

Get a FAITHFUL FRIEND

If you are very magnetic like me, it is **COMPLETELY** important to have a faithful friend, which is not the same thing as a scapegoat, and is also not the same as a dog, (especially not one that isn't yours but which you have found outside the post office only it is not lost at all) but e.g. Cosmo Moon Webster. Because faithful friends will always stand up for you, even when you have accidentally exploded custard in their microwave, and even if they are a boy and exactly a week older than you.

My
Faithful Friend

Joanna Nadin

wrote this book –
and lots of others
like it. She is small,
funny, clever,
sneaky and musical.

Before she became a writer, she wanted to be a
champion ballroom dancer or a jockey, but she
was actually a lifeguard at a swimming pool,
a radio newsreader, a cleaner in an old people's
home, and a juggler. She likes Marmite on toast
for mains breakfast, and jam on toast for
pudding. Her perfect day would involve baking,
surfing, sitting in cafes in Paris, and playing
with her daughter – who reminds her
a lot of Penny Dreadful...

marmite

Jess Mikhail

illustrated this book.
She loves creating funny
characters with bright
colours and fancy
patterns to make people smile.
Her favourite place is her tiny home, where she
lives with her tiny dog and spends lots of time
drawing, scanning, scribbling, printing, stamping
and sometimes using her scary computer. She
loves to rummage through a good car boot sale
or a charity shop to find weird and
wonderful things. A perfect day for
her would have to involve a sunny
beach and large amounts of curry
and ice cream (not together).

For Millie, Katherine and Freddie,
who are all magnets for disaster,
but not at all dreadful.

First published in the UK in 2011 by Usborne Publishing Ltd., Usborne House,
83-85 Saffron Hill, London EC1N 8RT, England. www.usborne.com

A CIP catalogue record for this book is available from the British Library.

ISBN 9781409526728   FMAMJJASOND/18   02349/25.

Printed in Chatham, Kent, UK.